Dinosaurs

By MARY ELTING
Illustrated by GABRIELE NENZIONI and MAURO CUTRONA
Consultant: KENNETH CARPENTER

A GOLDEN BOOK • NEW YORK
Western Publishing Company, Inc., Racine, Wisconsin 53404

 Library of Congress Catalog Card Number: 86-82160 ISBN: 0-307-11912-2/ISBN: 0-307-61912-5 (lib. bdg.)

The first dinosaurs that we know about lived almost 225 million years ago. The last ones died about 65 million years ago. Between those two times hundreds of different kinds of dinosaurs appeared on earth.

Dinosaur means "terrible lizard," and many of them *were* ferocious meat-eaters. They belonged to a group called theropods.

But most dinosaurs ate plants. The biggest of the plant-eaters were the gentle giants called sauropods. Other plant-eaters included the duck-billed dinosaurs (hadrosaurs); horned dinosaurs (ceratopsians); armored dinosaurs (ankylosaurs) and their relatives the stegosaurs; and many more. All of them were ancient relatives of crocodiles and other reptiles that live in the world today.

Nobody ever saw a live dinosaur. How, then, do we know they were real? Their bones tell us. When a dinosaur died, mud and blowing sand often covered its body. Its flesh decayed, and after a long time, the buried bones became as hard as stone. These stony pieces of dinosaurs are called fossils. Buried dinosaur eggs and even dinosaur footprints made in mud or sand became fossils, too.

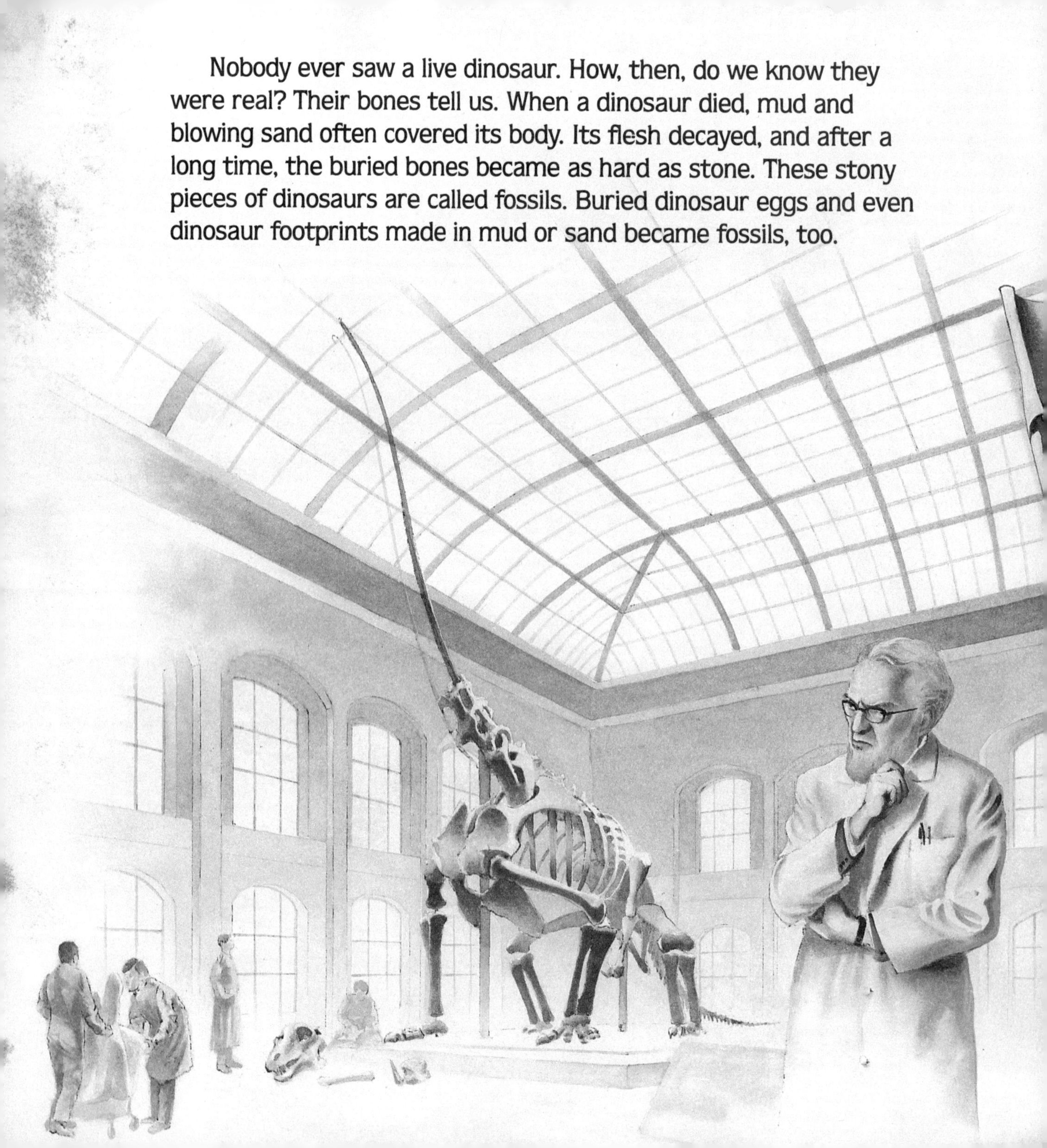

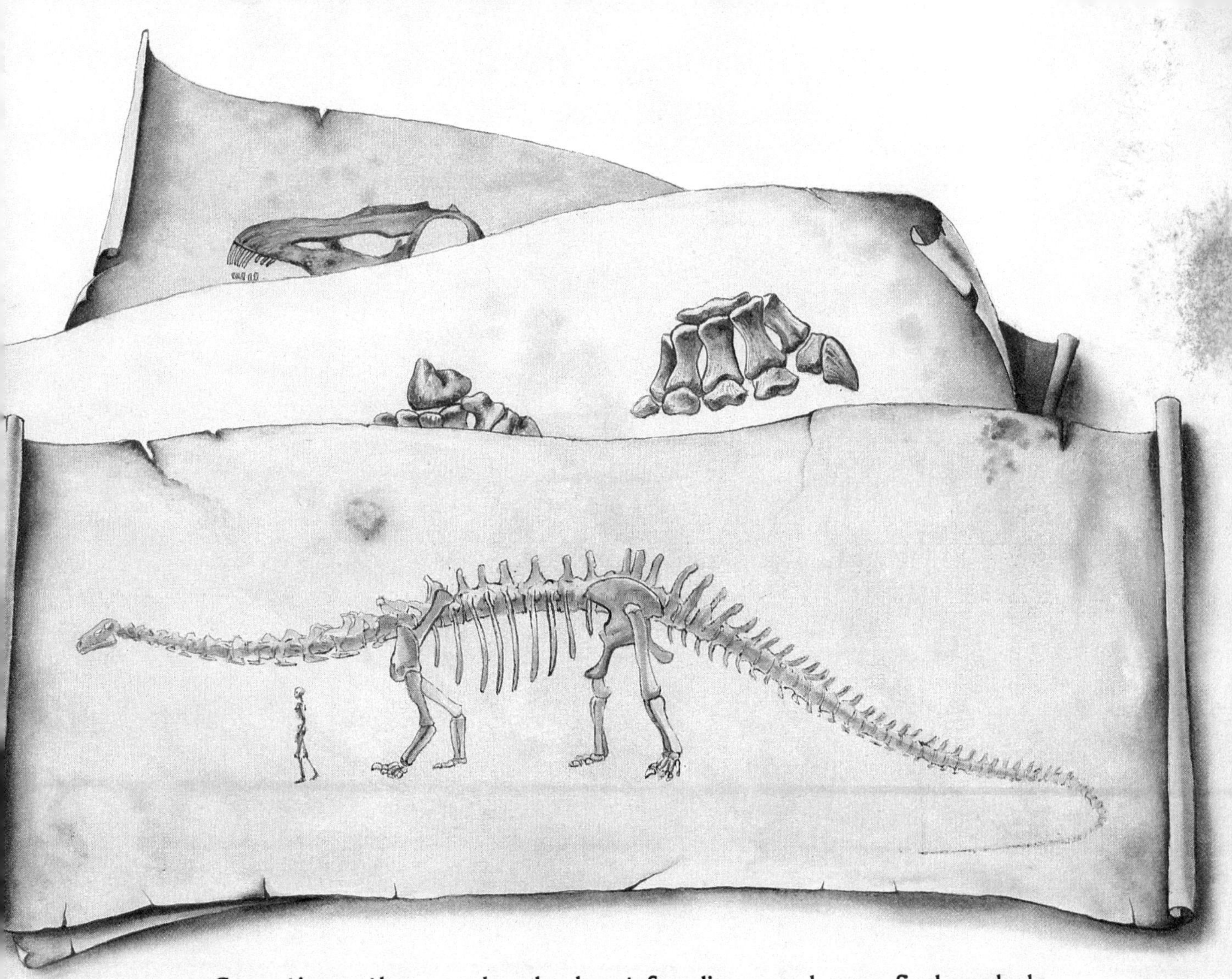

Sometimes the people who hunt for dinosaur bones find a whole skeleton with all the bones joined together. But usually the bones are all mixed up. Then someone has to figure out how to put the skeleton together. That isn't always easy. When the bones of a dinosaur called Diplodocus were discovered, some people thought they belonged to a giant creeping lizard. Yet scientists kept studying the bones. Finally they could tell how Diplodocus really looked when it was alive.

Diplodocus and its cousin Apatosaurus belonged to the group of dinosaurs that had very long necks. They were called sauropods. From the top of its head to the tip of its tail, Diplodocus was about 90 feet long. That is almost as long as three school buses. Diplodocus had the longest of all dinosaur tails.

Diplodocus

Diplodocus and the other sauropods had very small brains. Did this mean that they were stupid? People used to think so. But now scientists say that sauropods were smart enough to get along very well in the world as it was millions of years ago.

Apatosaurus may have had a shorter tail than Diplodocus, but its body was twice as heavy. In fact, Apatosaurus used to be called Brontosaurus, which means "thunder lizard," because of the noise its heavy feet must have made when it walked.

Apatosaurus

The skeleton of a sauropod called Brachiosaurus was 80 feet long and so tall, it could have rested its chin on the roof of a building four stories high. For a long time people thought it was the biggest dinosaur in the world.

Then Dr. James Jensen discovered bones that belonged to an even taller sauropod. He called it Ultrasaurus. It could have looked you in the eye if you were in a seat at the top of a Ferris wheel 60 feet high. Ultrasaurus probably weighed as much as 20 elephants.

Scientists hope to find the bones of an even bigger dinosaur called Breviparopus. So far they have discovered only the footprints it left in North Africa. How could fossil footprints tell its size? They are so big and so far apart that only a gigantic animal could have made them. Breviparopus may have been twice as long as Brachiosaurus.

Brachiosaurus

Now look at the fossil dinosaur footprint at the bottom of this page. It is actual size and the smallest one ever found. You could hold the tiny animal that made it in your hand. The birdlike shape of its toes tells scientists that this dinosaur walked on its hind feet.

Procompsognathus, which was about the size of a turkey, and Segisaurus, which was not much bigger than a goose, also walked on their hind feet.

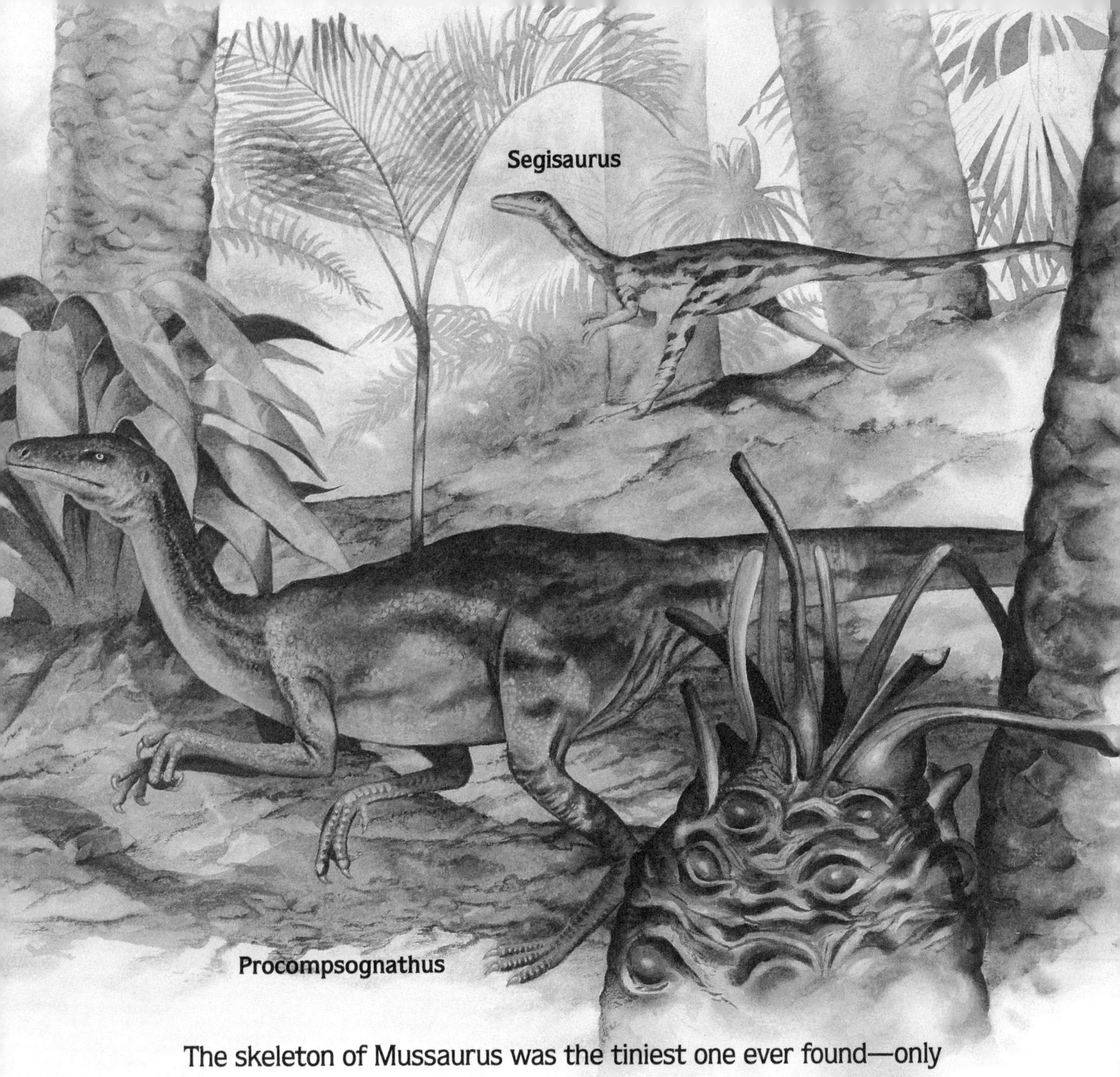

The skeleton of Mussaurus was the tiniest one ever found—only eight inches long. But scientists say it was just a baby dinosaur. How do they know? The bones and joints of a baby animal are not as well developed as those of an adult animal.

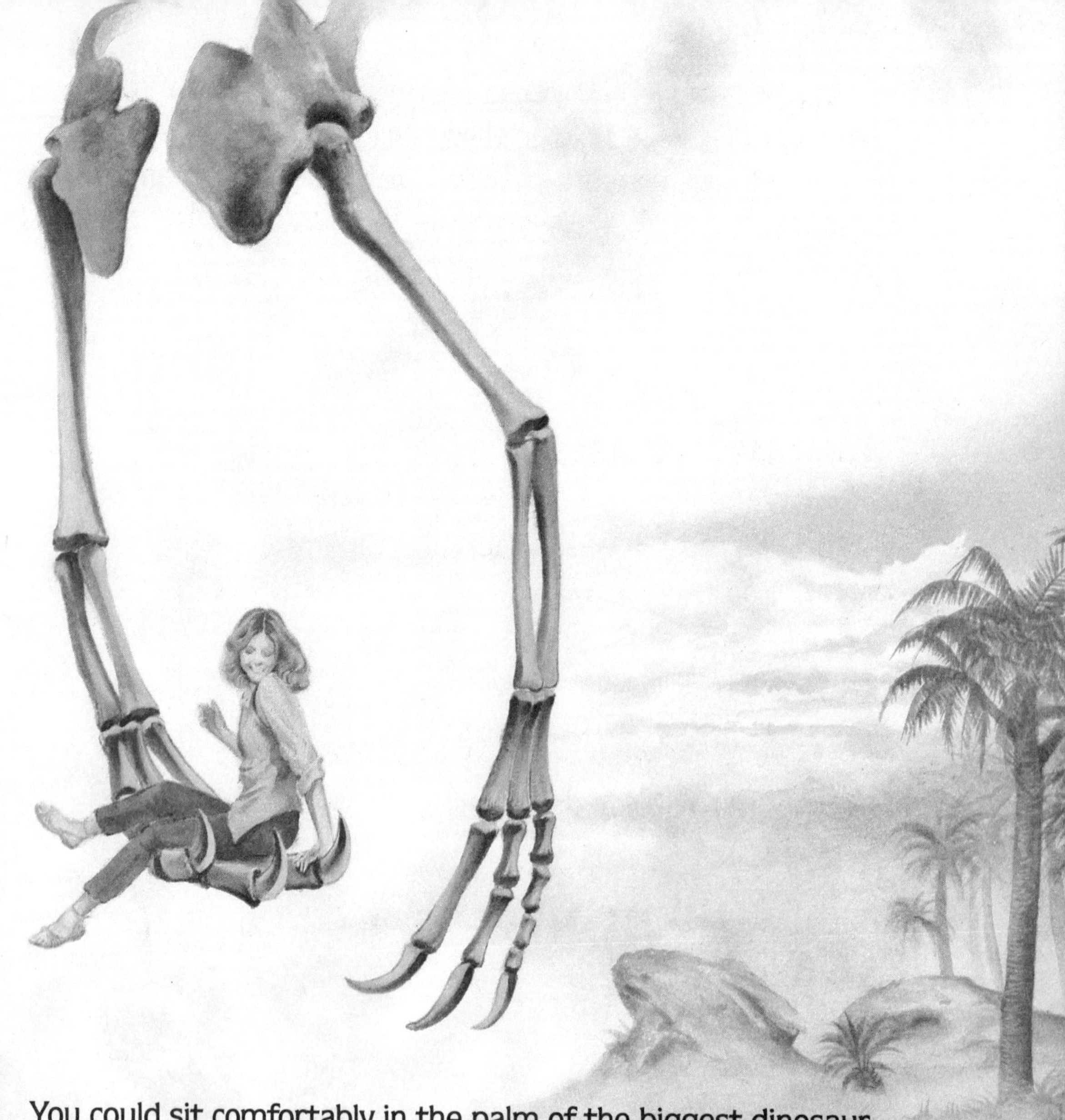

You could sit comfortably in the palm of the biggest dinosaur hand ever found. It belonged to giant Deinocheirus. The scientist who discovered the huge hand bones, arm bones, and claws never located the rest of the body, but she thinks Deinocheirus was a meat-eater. Why? The claws and arms are like those of Megalosaurus and other well-known meat-eaters.

A good way to tell whether a dinosaur was a meat-eater or a plant-eater is to look at its teeth. Plant-eaters had either flat grinding teeth, or teeth that cut like scissor blades and could mash and chop leaves, twigs, and fruit. Dinosaurs with long pointed teeth were meat-eaters called theropods.

Tyrannosaurus, one of the fiercest theropods, had teeth like huge daggers. Its jaws could open wide enough to take enormous bites that it swallowed in one gulp. If you could open your jaws the way Tyrannosaurus did, you could get a whole watermelon in your mouth.

Deinonychus was a small speedy theropod with a lot of teeth that had jagged edges like steak knives. The fingers on each of its hands ended in sharp claws. On the middle toe of each of its hind feet was a claw that could rip through the toughest hide. Whole bands of these ferocious little dinosaurs probably hunted together. When they found a big plant-eater, such as Iguanodon, they all leapt on it, biting and slashing with their terrible claws.

Stegosaurus had a strange shape, even for a dinosaur. The triangular plates on its back and neck were made of bone. Grooves in the plates may have held blood vessels, which could have made the plates work like radiators. On a hot day wind blowing over the plates would cool Stegosaurus by carrying heat away from its blood. The plates, along with spikes on Stegosaurus's tail, were probably scary enough to discourage any hungry meat-eater.

Stegosaurus was as big as a garbage truck. Its cousin Lexovisaurus, only half that large, had fewer plates on its back but many more sharp spines. A large spine, pointing downward, grew on each of its sides, just behind its hips. Another cousin, Dacentrurus, had no plates. Instead, two rows of dangerous-looking spikes stuck out all along its back.

Euoplocephalus

Ankylosaurs were also relatives of Stegosaurus. They had bony slabs like armor covering much of their bodies. Some ankylosaurs were as big as buses, and the smallest, called Minmi, was about the size of a bear. It had round chunks of bone under its skin for protection. Spikes on the sides of Edmontonia would have made it especially hard to eat. Euoplocephalus had an extra weapon. Its ten-foot-long tail ended in a huge bony knob. With one powerful swing of the tail, Euoplocephalus could break a meat-eater's jaw.

Dinosaurs called hadrosaurs had wide, rounded snouts like duckbills. In fact, "duckbills" is their nickname. Duck bills could probably swim if they had to escape from meat-eating theropods. But they could also travel quickly on dry land. How do we know? Their toes ended in small hooves, which were good for running.

Parasaurolophus

Some duckbills had skull bones with strange tall crests. What were they for? To explain them, scientists thought about the way duckbills lived. Great herds of them stayed together, just as different kinds of African antelope do today. The shape of an antelope's horns seems to help it recognize its own kind if it gets separated from the group. Perhaps the shape of a crest helped a lost duckbill in the same way.

Millions of dinosaurs called ceratopsians ("horned faces") once roamed the earth. Chasmosaurus and its many ceratopsian cousins carried around large bony slabs called frills that jutted out from the back of their skulls. The frill probably protected their necks. It also supported the enormous muscles that worked their powerful jaws and kept their heavy heads in place.

Torosaurus

Like the other ceratopsians, huge Torosaurus was a plant-eater. If Torosaurus leaned against a small oak tree, the trunk would snap. Then, with its scissor-like teeth, Torosaurus could chew the whole thing up, leaves, wood, and all.

Triceratops had a short frill, but its top horns were more than three feet long. They could have jabbed holes in a meat-eater's stomach. Even Tyrannosaurus probably hesitated to attack it.

Both Triceratops and Tyrannosaurus disappeared about 65 million years ago. After they died, there were no dinosaurs left anywhere on earth.

Triceratops

No one really knows why the dinosaurs vanished. Some scientists think that dinosaurs and other creatures disappeared after volcanoes erupted in many places. Clouds of ash from the volcanoes could have cut off sunlight and caused many plants to die. Without enough food, plant-eating dinosaurs would have died, too. The meat-eaters would then have quickly followed.

Other scientists think that a comet or a meteorite struck the earth and sent up clouds of dust that hid the sun. But perhaps other things killed the dinosaurs. Scientists are still looking for clues to the mystery. As they search they find out more about dinosaurs, too. Right now someone is probably digging up the bones of a new dinosaur that does not yet have a name.